THE MAN WHO LOVED LIBRARIES

The Story of Andrew Carnegie

Story by Andrew Larsen
Pictures by Katty Maurey

Owlkids Books

Andrew Carnegie was born
in a tiny stone cottage in a small
Scottish village.

A large wooden loom took up
most of the ground floor.

Andrew and his family lived, ate,
and slept upstairs in the attic.

Andrew's father was a weaver. But fewer and fewer people were buying the kind of fine linens he crafted on his loom. They wanted the newer, cheaper fabrics that were being made in mills.

To earn a little extra money, Andrew's mother sold candy, cabbages, and carrots from their cottage.

Young Andrew was hungry to learn.
He started going to a one-room
schoolhouse when he was eight.

The schoolmaster was strict.
Andrew liked that. He worked hard
to become an excellent student.

One evening, after yet another
meal of bread and carrots,
Andrew's father was gloomy.

"No one will buy my linens
anymore," he said.

"We have to do something,"
said Andrew's mother.
"My sisters have gone to America.
Perhaps we should go, too."

Andrew was twelve when his family set off for America. It was the perfect place for new beginnings.

The Carnegies traveled on a ship with many other immigrants. The food was foul, the air was stale, and the water was anything but fresh. Andrew and his younger brother Tom were too busy pretending to be pirates to notice.

After seven long weeks at sea, the Carnegies arrived in New York City. It took another three weeks to get to Pittsburgh, where Andrew's aunts had settled.

Pittsburgh was booming. The air was thick with the soot and smoke spewing from its many factories and mills.

There were plenty of jobs for newcomers.

Andrew went right to work to help support his family. He and his father found jobs at the Anchor Cotton Mills, where giant looms did the very work that Andrew's father had once done at home.

Andrew was a bobbin boy, scurrying around the factory floor, removing full bobbins from the machines and replacing them with empty ones. He worked twelve hours a day, with only short breaks for breakfast and dinner. It was hard work.

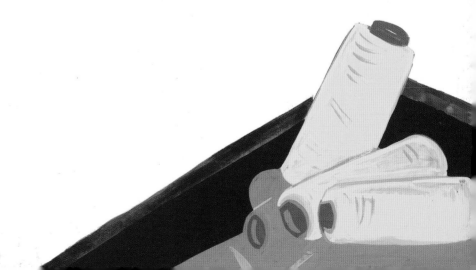

Within a year, Andrew found a new and better job. He became a messenger boy.

He studied street maps and learned the addresses of local businesses by heart so he could deliver telegrams lickety-split. He learned the names of the city's businessmen so they would get to know him. Andrew became one of the best messenger boys in all of Pittsburgh.

In his spare time, he learned
to operate the telegraph equipment.

Andrew knew that learning was the key to his future. He couldn't go to school because he had to work. He could read, but books were expensive. Pittsburgh, like most cities at the time, didn't have a public library where he could borrow books for free.

Luckily, there was someone who was interested in helping young workers to help themselves. Colonel Anderson, a local businessman, opened the doors to his own private library on Saturday afternoons.

Andrew loved Colonel Anderson's library. He loved its warmth and light. He loved to borrow the books that filled its shelves. He especially loved to read them.

The more he read, the more he learned.

When Andrew was seventeen, he used what he'd learned to get a job as a telegraph operator with the Pennsylvania Railroad Company.

He was going places!

He came up with new and exciting ideas, like keeping the telegraph office open twenty-four hours a day.

Andrew worked hard. By the time he was twenty-five, he was one of the bosses.

At the Pennsylvania Railroad Company, Andrew
earned enough money to support his entire family.
He was able to save a little bit, too! He invested
those savings and made even more money.

Andrew believed railroads were the key to the future. His first investment was with the Woodruff Sleeping Car Company. He went on to buy shares in companies producing oil and iron and steel, as well as those building the rails and bridges that were weaving their way across America. When they made money, he made money.

By the time he was thirty-five, Andrew Carnegie's investments had made him a rich man. He had more money than he could ever need. So what did he do?

He gave it away.

Andrew Carnegie never forgot the kindness of Colonel Anderson. He never forgot the light and warmth of the colonel's library or how he loved to borrow the books that filled its shelves. He never forgot the joy he felt in learning.

Andrew Carnegie used his own money to build public libraries so others could have the same opportunity.

He built his first public library in the small Scottish village where he was born. But he didn't stop there.

Andrew Carnegie built over 2,500 public libraries. He built them in cities, towns, and villages in the United States, Canada, and the United Kingdom. He built them in Europe, the Caribbean, Australia, and New Zealand. Many are still lending books today. In fact, there might be a Carnegie library near you.

Coming to America as a poor young immigrant, Andrew Carnegie grew up to become one of the richest people in the world.

He believed that riches are for sharing. He believed in helping others to help themselves. Andrew Carnegie built public libraries so that someday someone like you could feel the joy of borrowing a book like this.

Andrew Carnegie's Legacy

Andrew Carnegie was born in Dunfermline, Scotland, in 1835 and died in Lenox, Massachusetts, in 1919 at the age of 83.

Andrew Carnegie arrived in America in 1848 as a poor, young immigrant. He grew up to become one of the nation's richest citizens. Although he shaped the American steel industry, many believe his true legacy can be found in the numerous ways his charity continues to enrich our lives.

He set up the Carnegie Corporation of New York in 1911 to help promote peace and education around the world. This company is still doing important work. In fact, money from the Carnegie Corporation has been used to create education programs for kids and even helped put *Sesame Street* on television.

While he died long ago, Andrew Carnegie's money is still helping people. So is his story. It shows all of us that helping others is important, and that we can all make a real difference when we choose to give back.

Andrew was known to give generously to those in need. But his relationship with workers in his own factories was complicated. Carnegie Steel Company clashed many times with employees who banded together (or unionized) to fight for better working wages, hours, and conditions. The company crushed the steel workers' unions, and Andrew's business thrived. But his reputation as a working-class hero was never the same.

In 1892, the Carnegie Steel Plant in Homestead, Pennsylvania, was the site of a deadly union-busting conflict.

The Brooklyn Bridge, New York City

The Brooklyn Bridge was built with steel from Andrew Carnegie's company. Over 130 years later, the bridge is still standing. More than 120,000 cars, 2,600 cyclists, and 4,000 pedestrians cross it every day.

Andrew's wife, Louise, loved music. She and Andrew built Carnegie Hall as a place where musicians and other artists could perform. Carnegie Hall opened in 1891, and over 125 years later, it's still welcoming some of the world's greatest performers.

Carnegie Hall, New York City

This Carnegie Library opened in Revere, Massachusetts, in 1903 and is still in use today.

Andrew believed that the rich have a duty to use their money for the good of everyone. He started by building a library for the people in his hometown of Dunfermline, Scotland. Then he began to help other towns. If a community agreed to provide the money needed to buy books, pay staff, and maintain a library, then Andrew Carnegie would provide the money to build it. The community also had to agree that the library would be free to all.

Sources:

Carnegie Corporation of New York. "Andrew Carnegie's Story." Online.

Carnegie, Andrew. "Autobiography of Andrew Carnegie." Project Gutenberg. Online.

Davis, R. (Producer), & Perkins, J. (Writer). 1995. *Andrew Carnegie: Prince of Steel*. [Video]. United States: A&E Television Networks LLC.

Hoyt, Austin (Producer, Director, Writer). 1997. *The Richest Man in the World: Andrew Carnegie*. [Video]. United States: WGBH Media Library & Archives.

Nasaw, David. *Andrew Carnegie*. New York, NY: Penguin Books, 2007.

"People and Events: Andrew Carnegie." PBS.org, 1999. Online.

Simon, Charnan. *Andrew Carnegie: Builder of Libraries*. New York, NY: Children's Press, 1997.

Wall, Joseph Frazier. *Andrew Carnegie*. Pittsburgh, PA: University of Pittsburgh Press, 1989.

For librarians everywhere.
With special thanks to Monica Kulling for her continued inspiration. – A.L.

To all children's books authors and illustrators, past, present, and future. – K.M.

Text © 2017 Andrew Larsen
Illustrations © 2017 Katty Maurey

Photo Credits: 30: © Detroit Publishing Co., C. C. & Detroit Publishing Co., P., 1905; 31 (top): © Songquan Deng/shutterstock.com; 31 (middle): © Eddie Toro/Dreamstime.com; 31 (bottom): © Craig Hanchey

Owlkids Books acknowledges the financial support of the Canada Council for the Arts, the Ontario Arts Council, the Government of Canada through the Canada Book Fund (CBF), and the Government of Ontario through the Ontario Media Development Corporation's Book Initiative for our publishing activities.

Published in Canada by
Owlkids Books Inc.
10 Lower Spadina Avenue
Toronto, ON M5V 2Z2

Published in the United States by
Owlkids Books Inc.
1700 Fourth Street
Berkeley, CA 94710

Library and Archives Canada Cataloguing in Publication

Larsen, Andrew, 1960-, author
    The man who loved libraries : the story of Andrew Carnegie / written by Andrew Larsen ; illustrated by Katty Maurey.

ISBN 978-1-77147-267-8 (hardcover)

    1. Carnegie, Andrew, 1835-1919--Juvenile literature. 2. Industrialists-- United States--Biography--Juvenile literature. 3. Philanthropists--United States--Biography--Juvenile literature. 4. Carnegie libraries--Juvenile literature. I. Maurey, Katty, illustrator II. Title.

CT275.C3L37 2017   j338.7'672092   C2016-908272-5

Library of Congress Control Number: 2016962814

Edited by: Debbie Rogosin and Jennifer MacKinnon
Designed by: Danielle Arbour

Manufactured in Dongguan, China, in March 2017, by Toppan Leefung Packaging & Printing (Dongguan) Co., Ltd.
Job #BAYDC37

A   B   C   D   E   F

Publisher of Chirp, chickaDEE and OWL
www.owlkidsbooks.com

Owlkids Books is a division of